The Island of Slippery Souls

320 Sycamore Studios, Seattle Washington

For Jacob, whose enthusiasm kept me going.

—JW

To my parents, who always believed I had an artist's soul.

—KS

CONTENTS

A note to the reader VII

1. A fit of fidgets every Sunday 1
2. A home to every kind of person 4
3. Ellie's surprising soul 9
4. What about dung beetles? 12
5. King Clench thinks souls are far too unpredictable 16
6. The top of Tower Number 3 21
7. Ellie's there but not there 24
8. Monday morning: Clara's adventure begins 29
9. Monday evening: At the Scuttlebutt Saloon 34
10. Tuesday: The fish of the sea 38
11. Wednesday: The birds of the sky 42
12. Thursday: A beast of the earth 50
13. Can you ever hold onto a soul? 56
14. The mighty don't notice the small 65
15. A fit of fidgets every Sunday 71

A NOTE TO THE READER

Is a person a body?
Is a person a soul?
Is each part a part
of a greater whole?

Maybe we're neither,
it's hard to be sure.
Maybe we're both.
And maybe we're more.

1

A FIT OF FIDGETS EVERY SUNDAY

The fidgets started first with Clara Lightbody.

On this Sunday evening, just like every Sunday evening, the feeling began like flock of butterflies in her belly and finished with her toes twitching and tapping.

When the belly butterfly flutterby was done, Clara opened her eyes, smiled, and watched the three guests at her big maple table finish their own fidgets. She waited, excited to learn who they were this week.

It was Sunday afternoon on the Island of Slippery Souls, and Sunday afternoon was the time souls left one body and entered another.

2

A HOME TO EVERY KIND OF PERSON

Imagine an island so far away you think it only exists in the dreams of the people you dream of. It's a place ancient and distant and somehow familiar, with its its swelling green meadows, its dolphin-filled sea, and its tufts of puffed clouds scuffing by in the sky.

This is the Island of Slippery Souls, and it is a home to every kind of body.

There is a king and a queen. There are knights and nobility. Cats in the night and dogs with agility. Makers of crepes and tenders of grapes. Carpenters, caulkers, and high-wire walkers. Fishermen and fisherwomen, wisher men and washerwomen. Bank tellers and fortune-tellers. Melancholy babies (who are sad) and giddy babies (who are glad) and poopy babies (who stink real bad).

This is the Island of Slippery Souls, and it is a home to every kind of soul.

There are innocent souls and mischievous souls. Everyday souls, heroic souls, romantic souls, and stoic souls. Souls who like to break things, souls who like to make things, and souls who like to take and shake things. Some souls are magic. Some souls hold tight. Some souls are tragic. And some filled with light.

On the Island of Slippery Souls, there is room in a body for any kind of soul. And every body welcomes every kind of soul many times over. Because on the Island of Slippery Souls, every Sunday souls go on a walkabout. Every Sunday, bodies twitch, then souls switch. A body might be eating or napping or hoeing in the garden, when suddenly it feels a squirming, a fidget, a fit and...OUT goes one soul and IN comes another.

All across the island, bodies and souls were a joyful jumble, and life bumbled happily along.

For a while.

N
W
E
S

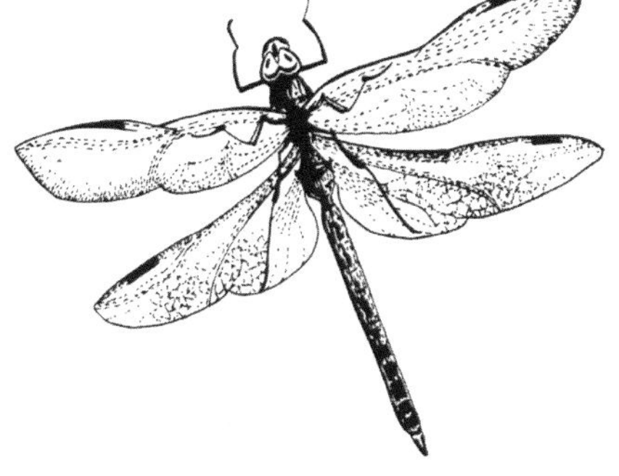

3

Ellie's Surprising Soul

Clara clapped her hands. "Well, tell me. Tell me! Who did you get? Son?"

"A regular old accountant this week, Mom." Ramon Lightbody looked intensely at his beans and began to count them.

"Why yes you did," she said. "You can learn a lot from everyday souls. How about you, Letitia?"

Clara's daughter-in-law paused a moment, holding her spoon in the air. "A doctor!" She turned to her mother-in-law. "Tell me, Clara, are you feeling well? Stick out your tongue."

"Ha! Put that spoon away. I'm quite well indeed!" Clara flexed her thin biceps. "I am a wandering monk." She got up to leave.

Letitia laughed and told her to at least save her wandering for after supper. She turned to her daughter, "And how about you, Ellie-girl?"

The nine-year-old girl looked dazed.

"Sweetie?" said Ramon, holding up his hand. "Everything alright? How many fingers am I holding up?"

Her voice was a whisper. "I'm the king."

"Ah," said Clara. "Your first! Well welcome back, your majesty."

"Be a good host to the king this week," said Letitia.

"As must we all to all!" said Clara. "Now, how about we enjoy the rest of our beans and greens and rutabaga stew and sweet potato chicken potpie while our bodies and souls get to know each other?"

"A toast," called Ramon, raising his glass of cool strawberry lemonade.

The others raised their lemonades.

"To flesh memories and soul stories, and flesh stories and soul memories."

4

WHAT ABOUT DUNG BEETLES?

One sunny Sunday afternoon several weeks later, Clara Lightbody crab-walked her way slowly along a row of rutabaga plants, sliding her nimble, weathered fingers gently up and down the tender vines. Now and then, she'd flick an aphid into the breeze or pause to pat-pat the soft soil.

Ellie watched her. "Your fingers are moving fast, yet you're precise with the soil, gentle with the insects, and quick with the weeds."

"Indeed," said Clara. "There's a weaver in me this time. These creative souls do suit the gardening. How about you, Darling?"

"A detective!" said Ellie.

Clara squinted at her and smiled. "Ah. Of course. You're very observant."

Clara turned back to her zucchinis.

A dung beetle lumbered out from under a leaf, patiently pushing a ball of poo. Clara picked up the beetle, held it in her palm, and blew on it till the awkward little fellow took flight.

Ellie watched the beetle disappear out over the pasture. "Why did you do that?"

"I thought he might like to go exploring," said Clara.

"Like a soul might." Ellie looked off toward where the beetle had flown. "What about them?"

"Hmm?" said Clara.

"Do they have souls? I never felt a dung beetle soul in my body."

"Well, it's only people who have souls, Sweetie."

Ellie frowned. "Not bugs?"

"Not bugs. Not trees or clouds or grass. Not any of the animals. Just like the people have a king, we are all kings over the fish and the fowl and the cattle."

"And bugs."

"That's right," said Clara.

"But it still doesn't make sense," said Ellie. "Maybe nobody ever told the bugs it was okay if their souls came in. Do you think it would work?"

"That's a very detective kind of question," said Clara. She thought a moment. "That would be a sight, wouldn't it? Do you think you'd want to suddenly start pushing around giant poo balls?"

They both laughed.

Ellie didn't get to try.

Just then her mother called her into dinner. After dinner, a very strange thing happened to her. And that very strange thing caused many other strange things to happen.

5

KING CLENCH THINKS SOULS ARE FAR TOO UNPREDICTABLE

That very same day, across the island, something unusual happened: The body of the king welcomed in the soul of the king.

It was a moment the kingbody had been waiting for, and it was the start of all the trouble.

Do you know about kings? Kings are silly creatures and can cause no end of problems if they aren't kept busy.

That was true of King Hieronymus Clench, who sat on his throne that Sunday, surveyed the great hall of his castle, and sighed a ridiculous sigh.

"What is it, Dear?" said the queen.

"What is it, Sire?" said his knights.

"What is it, Your Majesty?" said the lords and ladies of the castle.

The king made a sad face. "Subjects, a kingdom needs order if it is to prosper. However, our kingdom has a problem. It is far too unpredictable. Since the souls are the cause of this chaos..."

There was a terrible silence in the great hall.

"...they must be removed."

The great hall erupted in gasps. A serving boy, who'd just come in to refill the pitchers with cucumber water, gasped just to hear the gasping.

"Sire," sputtered the queen, "surely you have the soul of a trickster in you. The people are happy."

"I jest not!" shouted the king, rising to his feet. "They are happy, but they are not productive. A great kingdom is built on a foundation of endless glorious sameness! On our island, a body cannot make plans but that he has to change them every Sunday. A farmer should think only farming thoughts. A baker should think only baking thoughts. A wife should think only—"

"Wifing thoughts?" asked his wife.

"Exactly!" thundered the king.

The queen reached out and touched the king's arm. She spoke softly, "Just wait for your new soul. You'll see things differently." King Clench yanked his arm away. "I *have* been waiting, Queen, waiting for this day. Henceforth, I think only with my body."

The king scowled and flicked his wrist, dismissing the nobles.

The queen waited for the hall to empty. "'Think with your body.' What does that mean?"

"You'll know soon," he replied with a tight-lipped smile. "Quite soon."

K

K

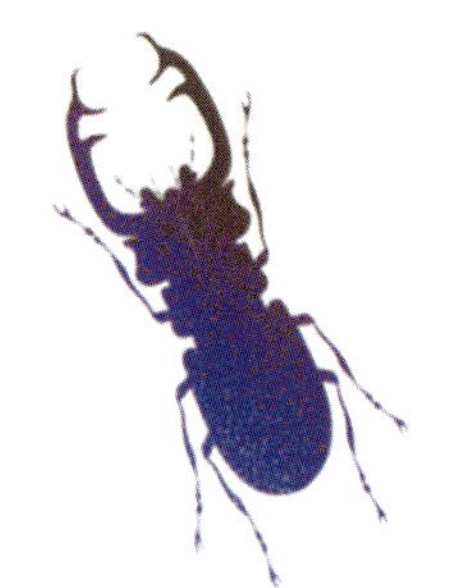

6

THE TOP OF TOWER NUMBER 3

That night the king crept to the top of the Tower Number 3. Around and around the narrow spiral staircase he went, up and up and up.

He stopped at last in front of a thick iron door, fished a key ring from his robe, and found key Number 3.

Insert. Twist. *Click click click* went the tumblers in the lock.

The great door creaked open, revealing a terrible room. A machine loomed out of shadow, all iron and brass and wire and glass. There was a control panel to one side, covered with switches and dials. There was a chair at the front of the machine, but it was no chair you'd ever want to sit in, not if you didn't want to feel its armstraps and legstraps tighten down around you. Behind the machine was a cylindrical storage tank, as tall as the king, with the word SOULS stenciled on one side. Extending from the back of the machine was an iron cone attached to a mechanical arm. The cone could be raised when not in use, or lowered like a hat onto the head of a person sitting in that awful chair. Coiled tubing ran from the top of the cone out through the roof.

King Clench clapped his hands three times in delight.
He pushed the door shut—*creaaaaak*—and locked it behind him—*click click click.*

On the side of the chair was a large knob with the following settings:

1. Collect one soul.
2. Collect all souls: Kids.
3. Collect all souls: Grown-ups (except king).
4. Collect all souls: Old people.
5. Make lemonade.

(The last one was a feature he added in case he got thirsty.)

The king turned the dial to setting 3. "Tempting," he whispered. "I could start right now."

"Best test it first," he decided. "I'll start with one. If that works, I'll harvest in waves."

King Clench turned the dial to 1 and flicked the machine ON. He plucked a brass wand from a holster in the side of the machine and clicked it into a wire. He pointed it off into the night. A slight humming, the whir of a fan kicking in, lights flickering on and off, and the machine sensors looked for a soul suitable for suction.

Suddenly the lights flashed on all at once, strong and steady. The machine had found a soul. King Clench made himself a glass of lemonade, and smiled.

7

ELLIE'S THERE BUT NOT THERE

Just as she did every Sunday evening, Clara Lightbody was reading in *Arrow's Poems for Gardeners.* Tonight, she was smiling over the poem on page 22, "Song of the Unsung Beetle of Dung," which began:

You, little farmers of the soil,
whose lives are filled with joy and toil.
Of you too seldom songs are sung.
But here's to all who roll the dung.

Her new soul, the soul of a pirate, chuckled inside her.

Clara heard screams.

"Clara! Clara!"

Letitia Lightbody's panicked cries shook Clara from her reverie. She snapped the book shut and rushed to her door.

Letitia stood on the front porch, panting.

Clara reached for her. "What? What?"

"Ellie—"

"What?"

"She's gone."

"Where?"

"No, she's in the house. I mean her body is. She's with Ramon. Oh Clara," Letitia's voice cracked, "It's like she's not there. Her soul is . . . gone."

Clara held her. "We'll put it right, child."

A few minutes later, Clara, Letitia and Ramon stood by Ellie's bed, peering down. Letitia held Ellie's hand. Ramon set a cool cloth on her forehead.

Ellie's eyes were open, but empty. She breathed fast shallow breaths.

"Tell me what happened," said Clara.

"It was suppertime—" mumbled Ramon.

"I'm so sorry I couldn't come this evening," interrupted Clara.

"It's okay, Mom. There's nothing you could have done. She let go of her explorer's soul. She was sad about it, I thought, but nothing out of the ordinary. After a little shake, she just went quiet..."

"And fell asleep," said Letitia. "We carried her to bed."

"We waited..." said Ramon.

"And then she woke up," said Letitia.

"Like *this*," said Ramon.

"That's when I came for you," said Letitia.

Clara knelt close, staring into Ellie's empty eyes.

"Ellie? Ellie child? Can you hear me?"

Nothing.

"Sweetie? Would you like to come garden with me tomorrow?"

Quick shallow breaths.

"Maybe we can find another dung beetle."

Suddenly, Ellie sat up and stared directly at Clara. "Remember the beetle," she rasped. Just as suddenly, she fell back into an impenetrable sleep. Outside the farmhouse, the

world was full of nightsound and moonlight and growing things.

"Maybe some tea . . ." whispered Clara, hardly knowing what to say.

The three of them sat at the kitchen table for a long time without speaking, barely sipping their cups of peppermint tea. Clara gazed out the window, across the pasture toward her own house, getting dim in the deepening gloom.

Ramon spoke softly. "I have an idea." He began to explain.

"You want me to go?" asked Clara.

Letitia squeezed her hand and said, "I can't bear to leave her."

"I can't either, Mother," said Ramon. "I can mind both farms."

"My body is so weak," said Clara.

"But your pirate soul is strong," said Letitia. "You told us yourself."

"Yes, you're right. Let me get my things." Clara pushed her chair back from the table.

"Wait till morning," said Ramon. "Let's give Ellie a good night's sleep. Just in case."

"Yes," said Letitia. "Maybe her soul got lost."

"I'm *sure* that's it," said Clara. "That *must* be it."

8

MONDAY MORNING: CLARA'S ADVENTURE BEGINS

Clara hurried back at daybreak, clutching her battered carpetbag. The bag didn't weigh much—she'd only brought an extra pair of overalls, her copy of *Arrow's Poems for Gardeners*, and a bundle of dried rutabaga knotted into a handkerchief.

Ramon and Letitia pushed the door open. They were pale.

"No change?" asked Clara.

They shook their heads.

"You were up all night, weren't you?"

They nodded.

At that moment, the world decided to string a series of jewels onto the necklace of dawn. Soft buttery light. Spangles of dew on the pasture. A symphony of birdsong in the trees.

The universe was briefly beautiful, and then the jangle of a bugle overran the moment.

A messenger rode into the yard, dressed in purple and red, the colors of the king. He brought his breathless horse skidding to a halt in the yard. He didn't say good morning. He simply pulled a scroll from his velvet vest.

"A proclamation from the king concerning souls," he said in a bored voice.

As they are known to cause
disorder,
and as disorder is the enemy
of any productive body politic,
be it hereby and henceforth proclaimed
to all citizens
that for their own good and happiness,
all souls will be gathered and detained
for further observation
until such time it is determined
that they may once again inhabit
our bodies and our kingdom
without threat of further disorder.

Clara was outraged. "That is ridiculous and it is impossible! Rounding up souls! I never heard such a thing."

The messenger ignored her.

Collection of souls will begin
immediately.
Now that we know
initial test results have been...

The messenger looked down his nose and frowned.

...successful.
Collection will progress from young to old,
in three successive harvests. We begin tomorrow, Tuesday morning, and the process
will be complete at dusk three days from now—
Thursday night.
Please make ready.
Order is law.
Law is duty.
Duty is good.
Good is order.
And so on.
Harboring souls will henceforth
be punishable by prison.
Long live the king's body!

The messenger rolled up the scroll and galloped away, but not before his tired horse gave a sympathetic look back at the Lightbodys.

Clara, Letitia, and Ramon staggered over to the porch swing and sat down, dazed. Hands fumbled for hands. Cheeks pressed into cheeks. There was a cough from the house. They rushed inside.

Ellie was sitting in her bed.

“Good morning, Mother. Good morning, Father. Hello, Grandma Clara.”

“The king’s plan failed!” said Clara.

Ramon and Letitia hugged their daughter.

Ellie patted their backs mechanically.

“Ellie, are you okay?” Letitia held her daughter’s shoulders and stared into Ellie’s eyes. Her empty eyes.

“Yes, Mother. Whysoever do you ask? I did have the strangest dream. I could do anything I wanted—play, wander, dream. It was terrible. So unproductive.” Ellie blinked slowly. Once. Twice. “Thank goodness it was just a dream. I must get to my chores.”

“Ellie,” whispered Clara. “What about the dung beetle?”

“Messy, messy creatures.”

Ellie rose from her bed and lurched past them. They heard the front door open and close.

Clara hugged her son and daughter-in-law.

“Mind my rutabagas. If the king will not listen to me,” she smacked a fist into her palm. “I will force him to.” And with that, she began her journey.

She had three days.

9

MONDAY EVENING: AT THE SCUTTLEBUTT SALOON

Clara's beloved farm boots got a workout as she walked the peaceful miles into Stumbletown, the nearest port village. She passed farms in the full glory of morning. Rows of sunflowers turned their faces to the sun. Horses nickered in the fields. Honeysuckle flowers perfumed the pastures. Ants built tiny empires by the roadside. The sweet melody of life.

There was so much goodness in the world. Clara opened to it like a sunflower herself, body and soul. She drank in the world, and the world filled her with strength.

She would need it.

It was a full day's walk and the sun had set by the time she arrived at the door of the Scuttlebutt Saloon. A creaking wooden sign hung above the entrance. There was a water barrel carved into it, and these words:

The Scuttlebutt

Where sailors come
to get their fill
of talk and grog,
for good or ill.

She narrowed her eyes and pushed through the door.

Grizzled faces in the shadows. Flickering candles jammed into cracked whiskey bottles. Tables stained with slime, grime, and time. Strong shoulders bent by years of leaning into hard weather. Grumbled conversations over mugs of suds. A wizened sailor cradled a flagon of grog in a corner, smoking a foul-smelling pipe and singing softly to himself:

Some people claim that I'm touched in the head.
They say don't worry, for we'll soon be dead.
I tell them rubbish! You go hang your dread!
I see seabreezes and full sails ahead.

Clara would have been inspired if he hadn't toppled off his stool onto the ale-sticky floor and fallen fast asleep.

Clara stepped nervously to the bar. A bald and bearded mountain of a man eyed her from behind the counter. Tattoos of sea monsters twisted up and down his thick forearms. One of his ears was missing.

He spat a glob of tobacco juice onto the floor behind the bar. "Good Monday evening to you, ma'am," he said cheerfully. "Bartender Joseph's who I am. It looks like you've had quite a walk. Perhaps you'd like to sit and talk?"

Clara was confused, for a moment. It's strange how even after a lifetime of practice, you can still judge a person by how they look on the outside instead of by the soul on the inside. She collected herself and smiled. "Soul of a—"

"Poet," he beamed. "Wouldn't ya know it? It's me first. Do ya thirst?" He hunched over the bar and leaned close. "It's right unwearying, somehow, to have a poet so close now. It's sure been a downright troublesome day. We all need a story to light the way."

"I do need some unwearying," sighed Clara.

Bartender Joseph beamed. "Well, let this be the end of your trip. Care for whiskey? Rum?"

"A ship."

All the scuttlebutt in the Scuttlebutt stopped.

"A ship?"

"For Clenchport."

"Clenchport?"

"Aye."

Bartender Joseph shook his great bald head and frowned. "But why?"

The singing sailor on the floor woke up. "I kin take ye."

10

TUESDAY: THE FISH OF THE SEA

The wind started blowing fierce the moment Captain Barnacle Bennick's little sailboat cleared the Stumbletown breakwater.

Clara had to shout to be heard. "Will the ship hold, Captain Bennick?"

"Call me Barnacle!" he shouted back. He squinted into the squall and puffed his pipe. Clara was glad to be upwind of it. "And, aye, she'll hold. Been through worse."

The ship held, but only till late afternoon.

All day the wind got windier, and the rain got rainier, and the waves got wavier. The little old boat strained heroically up the faces of the swells and skittered down the backs, but after a while the struggle was all too much.

She gave up all at once and sank right down, leaving spare sails and oars and casks and flasks scattered about the surface.

Clara and Captain Bennick barely had time to leap over the rail before the ship disappeared into a heap of feeble bubbles.

They struggled a while in the waves. Clara, with her wiry pirate strength, supported the captain. But the waves battered even her stout soul, and she grew weary. Clara thought of Ramon and Letitia, poor Ellie and all the children who would be just like her at dusk. What would happen to them now? She gave the captain's hand a squeeze and said, "Fare thee well, Captain."

"Fare thee well, Clara." Captain Bennick chewed his soggy pipe. "You're a good woman. I regret I met you too late."

The bubbles burbled over their chins.

The foam rose over their noses.

The sea surged over their heads.

And then...

They were lifted from below.

Just like that, they were rising. They were moving. They were speeding along above the surface of the waves. Joyous, Clara held the fin beneath her and patted the smooth skin of a dolphin.

"Whee-hee!" she shouted into the spray, glancing at Captain Barnacle, who was trying to look dignified atop his dolphin. The dolphins surged through the sea, racing them up to the closest stretch of land—an isolated crescent of a beach nestled at the base of a high cliff.

Clara and Captain Barnacle swam through the shorebreak and collapsed on the beach at dusk, happy for the moment their bodies were still alive.

They slept through the night.

When they woke in the morning, Clara was astonished to see the waves had deposited her soggy carpetbag on the sand.

She reached inside and untied the bandanna holding the dried rutabaga. She waded into the waves a short way and threw the vegetables into the water.

11

WEDNESDAY: THE BIRDS OF THE SKY

Gulls wheeled over the beach, singing the praises of morning.

Clara nudged Captain Barnacle awake.

They surveyed their surroundings.

"Pretty stretch of beach," she said, taking off her farm boots and wringing out her socks.

"Oh, aye," growled the captain looking sadly at his soggy pipe. "It's Unlucky, though."

She punched him gently on the shoulder. "Well, I *know* that."

He squinted at her. "No, that's its name. Unlucky Beach."

Pretty as the beach was, with its soft auburn sand and fringes of lantern trees, Unlucky Beach indeed was bound all around by high cinnamon-colored cliffs.

The gulls didn't mind of course. They called to each other merrily in their ragged voices.

Clara put on her socks and shoes and scanned the beach. "Can we swim 'round the headland, Barnacle?"

"Dangerous currents."

"Climb the cliffs?"

"Too high."

"Hail a passing ship?"

"The captains are all hunkering down, waiting for the soul collection."

"Argh. Is there no one to help us? And why aren't the boat captains doing something?"

"When a storm's coming, you hunker down, try to ride it out," he said.

"But *you* didn't."

"I like storms," he said.

"Well I do, too," said Clara.

Clara marched across the sand to the base of the nearest cliff. Rock chunks broke off in her hand when she tried to climb. Grumbling, she marched along the beach, looking for a rib of rigid stone or a braid of dangling roots, anything she could ascend by.

Captain Barnacle plodded up the shore, inspecting the line of driftwood to see if anything the ocean had brought in could provide the means of a seaward escape.

So passed a long and fruitless day.

All the while, the gulls busied themselves around a deep heap of seaweed at the center of the beach, just at the high-tide line. They'd pluck at the damp clump, tease out long kelpy strands, and lay them in lines.

Finally, as the sun was drawing low, Clara harrumphed, crossed her arms and leaned back against the defective cliff. A clod broke loose and plonked her on the head.

"Grr."

Captain Bennick came up at last to meet her. "Anything?"

She shook her head. "You?"

"No." He sat down against the cliff and gazed out to sea.

She sat down next to him. "It'll be a good sunset, though," she said. The breeze had died away, and the waves made a gentle symphony on the shore. The gulls still intent on their pile of kelp, though it was much smaller now.

"Aye. A good one to end on."

She looked at him a long minute, then saw how young he was under his wrinkles.

"I know we can't choose our time," he said, meeting her gaze. "But I always did want to give farming a try. I think it would have suited me."

Clara swallowed. "But, I'm so much older."

"Not all that much. Besides, I think our souls would have gotten along. All of them."

Suddenly the entire flock of seagulls took off at once and flew toward them, screaming.

The gulls stopped short and fell silent. Just as suddenly, they flew back to their seaweed, stopped, and looked back at Clara and the captain.

Clara noticed that the seaweed pile was now completely gone. Clara got up and took a step forward, curious. Then another. The gulls cawed encouragement.

The captain rose. He and Clara jogged over to the gulls. They stopped, puzzled.

The gulls had spent the day arranging the seaweed carefully so now the strands of it lay in hundreds of neat rows.

"Well, I've never . . ." began the captain. But he was unable to finish the sentence.

A small squad of gulls took noisily to the sky, flew to the clifftop edge, and perched there, squawking.

Clara squinted up at them. Then back to the seaweed. She understood.

"Captain! Start tying the strands together. Hurry, we've no time to lose."

They went to work knotting the strands together, racing the sinking sun. When they finished, the strands had become one very long rope. Long enough to reach a good way up the beach.

Or down a cliff.

The gulls wasted no time. They clamored to the kelp-rope. Each bird took a length in its beak, and with mouths full, they flew upward as one. The gulls were beautiful as they rose, a great feathered kelp-scarf silhouetted against gold light turning red turning purple.

The gulls looped the rope at its midpoint around a stout sea pine and let it fall all the way back down the cliff face—one very long rope that looked like two. The gulls released a chorus of triumphant squawking.

Clara spat on each hand and clapped twice.

"Well I'll be a barnacle's blowhole," said the captain.

Clara tugged the rope.

The captain cleared his throat. "Sun's almost down. We'd best get on."

"One moment!" Clara rushed to her carpetbag on the beach. She took out her book of poems and her pair of overalls and stuffed them into her jacket. She carried the empty carpetbag to the base of the cliff, opened it up, and set it under a pretty little lantern tree.

She addressed the seagulls. "This will make a lovely nest for one of you. Thank you, birds of the air."

Time to climb. Up up up went Clara and the captain and down down down went the sun. The rope flexed with the weight of their climbing but held fast.

"Captain?" asked Clara as they neared the top.

"Barnacle," he interrupted.

"Barnacle," she corrected herself. "I never asked you. What's your soul this week?"

Clara cleared the cliff-edge first and reached down a hand to the captain.

Just in time.

The moment she pulled him clear he began to shiver. He staggered to a clearing under a tree, a safe distance from the cliff edge. The pipe fell from his mouth to the grass.

His eyes rolled. He only had strength enough to whisper.

"A romantic."

Clara held his hand as his soul was wrenched from his body.

When it was done, his empty eyes didn't see her anymore. He opened his mouth to speak, but no words came out. He drifted off to sleep.

Clara was alone.

She had a terrible thought. *What if I am the last one on the island with a soul?*

"Oh, Captain," she said. "I regret I didn't meet you sooner, too. But maybe it's not too late."

Clara took her wadded overalls out of her jacket and rolled them into a pillow for the captain. He looked comfortable, but something was still wrong. She thought a moment.

"Ah!" She set the captain's pipe between his teeth and shut his jaw. "That's better."

She tucked his pea jacket snug around him and kissed his forehead.

"You sleep now, Barnacle. I'll do my best."

She walked half the night through the woods, until, overcome with emotion and exhaustion, she collapsed into tumultuous sleep.

At dawn of the third day, the most important day of all, she woke to mooing.

12

THURSDAY: A BEAST OF THE EARTH

Clara let the farm sounds guide her—mooing, whinnying, bleating, cluck-clucking, and scraps of human voices floating on the wind. She soon crested a rise and came out of the woods to the edge of a farm.

A man spotted her and called his family to him. They were still, silent, watching as she skirted the pasture fence and approached. She waved hello. No one waved back.

It was a young family, a husband, wife, two boys and two girls. All with vacant eyes. Ellie's eyes.

Is this how Ramon and Letitia look now? thought Clara. *Yes, it must be.* She swallowed.

"Good day," she said.

"What's your business?" asked the father.

"My business. Ah...I'm on my way to see—"

Suddenly, Clara didn't think it was wise to tell them that she was on her way to see the king and put a stop to this whole soul-snatching business.

"I've run into a spot of trouble and need to get to town. I was wondering if I might, if I might borrow a horse."

"No borrowing," said the man. "You can rent." The woman frowned. The children scowled.

"Well, any money I had is at the bottom of the sea. But I desperately need to travel to Clenchport by sundown. It's for, it's for— "

"Business?" asked the farmer

"Chores?" asked the children.

"Yes," said Clara. "Both."

"No money, though?"

"No."

"Can't help ya," said the father. "Now we best be to our work. Time is money, and you've cost us plenty already. Git along, kids."

With that, Clara was abandoned. She started walking.

In spite of everything, her soul delighted in the glory of the morning. The butterflies, the music-box tinkle of a little stream, the sweet smell of wheatgrass. Slowly, though, she became aware of a presence, a shadow behind the roadside hedge, moving alongside her.

Clara stopped, stooped, and pretended to tie up a bootlace.

The shadow stopped.

Clara walked on.

The shadow walked on.

Clara's heart began to beat a little faster. She began to trot. Up ahead, she saw a break in the hedge, a gate, and open road beyond.

The massive shadow trotted with her.

Heart pounding, Clara sprinted down the lane. As she raced past the gate, she turned her head and saw the inky dark face of a massive bull. He gave a fantastic snort!

Clara stopped and put her hands on her hips.

The bull was as tall as she was. His head was sleek and black and magnificent. He snorted again, more softly. He watched her. For all his ferocity, there was an intelligence in his eyes.

"You scared me!" Clara harrumphed, turning to leave.

The bull bellowed.

"What!"

The bull nuzzled the gate latch.

"You want out? I don't think the farmer would like that."

The bull nosed the latch again.

"You know," she said, "I don't think I much care what the farmer thinks."

She opened the gate and waited for the bull to run off.

The bull stepped out of the pasture and stopped in the lane next to Clara.

"Go on," said Clara.

The bull snorted again and tossed his head. "Oh," said Clara, suddenly understanding.

The bull was inviting her to ride.

So she did.

Clara rode through the jangling, jouncing morning and arrived at a hill on the outskirts of Clenchport late that afternoon.

Clara slid down and threw her arms around the bull's neck. He nuzzled her. When Clara stepped back, he'd plucked *Arrow's Poems for Gardeners* out of her jacket and was happily munching away.

“Hey,” she started. “Oh, go ahead! Poems *are* good food.”

Clara kissed the bull on his velvety nose. He trotted off, chewing poetry.

Clara thanked the strength of her pirate soul for getting her this far.

But she would need even more from it. A lot more.

13

CAN YOU EVER HOLD ONTO A SOUL?

King Clench stood at a castle balcony and surveyed his realm. His kingly soul was stuck in his kingly body, just as the souls of the children and the grown-ups were stuck tight in the soul storage tank in Tower Number 3.

The streets below him were quite orderly. The gentlemen greeted the ladies, the ladies tended the children, and the children walked quietly and politely behind their parents. Carriages proceeded quietly down the street, and any time a horse pooped, an attendant rushed to scoop it into a bin. Parks were quiet. Hymns in the cathedral were subdued. Ships floated neatly at the wharf.

The Old People's Home on the edge of town was safely locked up—from the outside. The king patted the key in his pocket and smiled. Tonight his work would be complete. Tomorrow would mark the start of the kingdom of predictability.

The king felt a hand on his shoulder.

"Ah, my Queen," he beamed. "Do you like our kingdom now?"

"It changed," she said in a spiritless voice. "It's so very predictable, now. Not like before." He looked into her empty eyes, her beautiful empty eyes.

"Yes," he said, looking back over the town. "Change IS good. When it brings sameness."

"Is it done?" asked the queen.

The king didn't answer. Something caught his eye. A lone figure marching down the center of Castle Road, not walking on the right side of the street. Not walking in a straight line. And certainly not going quietly.

No, not quietly at all.

Clara Lightbody dashed from one side of the street to the other. Stomping and shouting and making all manner of noises to rouse her fellow citizens.

She chittered like a dolphin. She screamed like a seagull. She bellowed like a bull.

The people ignored her.

She shouted a sea shanty, just like Captain Barnacle Bennick. She sang it LOUD, with a pirate's spirit.

Come with me people, ye mighty and low.
Come down from your rooftops, climb out of your holes.

Come as you are, you fast and you slow.
Come with me now to reclaim your souls!

She scampered about. She tugged the sleeves of passersby. The men, the women, the children. The high and the low. But they had no souls to give them direction. They simply scoffed, slid by, and walked on.

It was the third day. The sun was dropping.

Clara stopped in the middle of the street. She threw up her hands and cursed. "Ack! Where are the other old ones, like me?"

She felt a terrible angry strength surge through her, body and soul. Her body fed off all the bad feelings it felt, and her strong soul thrilled with power.

Clara Lightbody stood tall and screamed at the king on his balcony.

"I'm coming for you, King!" She ran toward the castle gates.

The king turned to his queen. "You asked me if it was done."

She nodded.

"It will be soon."

Clara rounded a corner and saw the open castle portcullis ahead of her. She ran faster than she had in years, thanking the strength of her soul.

The gatekeeper saw her coming. "Lower the gate! Now!" he shouted.

The portcullis creaked downward.

The king's soldiers poured out of the guardhouse in front of the castle wall and jogged toward Clara. Their lines were very orderly.

The shadows grew longer.

Clara raced at the soldiers.

The soldiers raced at Clara.

Closer, closer . . . CRASH!

They collided before the gate. The soldiers never had a chance. They flew into the air like bowling pins, landing scattered on the street.

"Sorry!" she called, sprinting ahead. The gate was almost down.

"Oh no," Clara lunged, and just managed to get her fingers underneath the portcullis.

Her biceps flexed. Her legs strained. Her eyes bulged to bursting. Clara fought gravity mightily and inch by inch began to lift the gate.

The gate rose slowly.

To her ankles.

Behind her, the scattered guards moaned and gathered themselves.

To her knees.

In front of her, castle guards poured shouting into the courtyard.

To her waist.

It would have to do. The soldiers were charging again from behind.

Clara dropped and rolled under the gate, into the castle courtyard. The gate slammed shut behind her, just as the soldiers reached it.

Clara faced the inside guards. They arranged themselves in a semicircle around her, spears lowered.

"Halt this nonsense!" called a voice. King Clench. He stood on the top step of the castle doorway. "I see you've come for me indeed."

"King!" said Clara. "I demand you free the souls! Please . . ."

The shadow of evening crept up the stairs and to his feet.

"My dear woman, the changes I have brought are to make our island better, more orderly. For it is by order that we prosper."

The shadow rose toward his face.

"It's not right."

The king raised an eyebrow. "Oh?"

"You've stolen the joy," said Clara.

She wobbled.

"Order *is* joy," said the king. "Order is the *best* thing."

"But it's so . . . empty," murmured Clara. Then she fell.

Clara drifted in a misty dreamscape. Somewhere, deep inside herself, she remembered a conversation with Ellie.

"Can you ever hold on to a soul?"

"Oh I suppose, perhaps, if you squinched yourself up real good."

The king clapped twice. "Carry the body to the throne room," he commanded.

Clara's body did not move as it was lifted and carried into the castle, along the great hallway, up the broad stone stairs, and past the vacant faces of the gathered nobility.

Clara's body did not move as the soldiers set her down in the middle of the throne room.

Clara's body did not move as the king began to speak.

"It is a blessed day for the Island! We've cleaned out the souls and created order!"

The room resounded with hollow hurrahs and hip-hip-hoorays.

Then Clara's body did move. Fast.

She dashed across the stone floor, bounded up the steps to the throne, and wrapped the king in a massive bear hug. She squeezed him hard—so hard he farted. Screams and wails rebounded around the room.

The castle guards raced toward their king.

"Halt!" shouted Clara.

The guards halted.

"I'll squeeze the life right out of him!"

There was silence, then into the silence came an unexpected sound.

The king was laughing.

"What are you laughing about?" she asked.

"I sense in you a kindred body," said the king.

"I'm nothing like you," hissed Clara.

"You held your soul, did you not?"

"Yes, to stop you."

"Because you knew you could not get what you want by letting go."

"But—" Clara began.

"You became just like me. You kept your soul because you know life requires mastery, control, dominion—and order!"

"No, I'm not like you," Clara stammered. But she felt confused, and in her confusion, the king broke free from her.

Clara was soon back in the clutches of the castle guards.

"Take her to Tower Number 3," the king commanded.

The guards carried her up the narrow spiral stairs and through the brute iron door. They wrestled her into the terrible chair. The king himself pulled the metal cap of the soul machine down onto her head.

The last thing Clara saw was the tank labeled SOUL STORAGE. Then her world went dark.

The king lifted Clara's eyelids with his thumbs. "You'll wake soon enough," he said. "And when you do, you'll understand dominion. The dominion that I now have over you and the fish and the birds and the beasts—over every living thing."

The king unbuckled her from the chair and bid the guards take her away.

They carried Clara's body from the highest part of the castle to the lowest, down below the pantries and larders and the rum cellars and upper dungeons to the lower dungeon.

And so it was that Clara Lightbody's journey brought her to a muddy, lonely dungeon cell at the bottom of the castle on the Island of Not-So-Slippery Souls.

14

THE MIGHTY DON'T NOTICE THE SMALL

Three days passed in the lonely dungeon cell before Clara groaned awake.

"Where am I?" she asked the walls. "I do not know this place. It is so messy. I must clean it."

Clara got to her feet, but quickly slid to the floor. She called out. "Hello?"

Clara felt immensely sad, but she wasn't sure why. "Maybe I deserve to be here." She folded her hands on her lap and tried to imagine what had brought her here.

She felt a tickle on the back of her right hand and twitched.

"This is all right and orderly. It must be so. So why am I so sad? What's wrong with me?

I should feel happy."

She felt the tickle again on her right hand. Clara looked upward and said to nobody, "What should I do?"

The tickle again. "What is this?" she asked. She held her wrist up to her face. Something was perched there waggling its stubby little antenna. An insect. A beetle.

A dung beetle.

A phrase floated into her brain, a thin wisp of flesh memory.

Remember the beetle.

"Where does that come from?" she asked the air.

Ellie.

"Who is Ellie?"

She's family.

"What else did Ellie say?"

I think the animals have souls, too. You just have to let them in.

Those words were like a key unlocking the universe to Clara. Suddenly, she remembered everything. Who she was. What was happening. How she'd gotten here.

Clara held open her vest pocket and set the beetle in. She patted the floor and felt around for a poo pellet, and she dropped it in her pocket.

And then Clara Lightbody lay back upon the foul earth at the bottom of the kingdom and relaxed her body, and she said to the beetle, "Please come in."

The feeling began like flock of butterflies in her belly and ended with a twitching tapping in her toes. Soon, she welcomed in a new soul.

Of a shepherd dog.

She sat up, astonished. "A dog? ...Of course, why would the body of a beetle have the soul of a beetle?"

At that moment, the dung beetle said hello to the soul of a cockatoo, a clever bird that is very good at picking locks.

The beetle crawled out of Clara's pocket, across the floor, and up the bars of the cell door. He went to work.

A short time later, Clara was racing to the top of Tower Number 3. Around and up she sped until finally, she came to the great iron door.

She smacked right into King Clench.

The guards soon had her strapped into the soul sucker once again.

King Clench shook with rage. "I don't know how you did it, but you aren't going to create disorder ever again. After we extract your soul, we're putting you in the bottomest of the secret lower dungeons. No body—or soul—gets out."

The dung beetle crawled out of Clara's pocket, down her sleeve, and into the keyhole of the soul storage tank.

The king didn't see the beetle.

The mighty don't notice the small.

King Clench directed the captain of the guard to flip the switch of the soul machine. Clara closed her eyes. The machine whirred. When it hummed to a stop, Clara blinked. The king leaned in. His nose touched hers.

Clara took a deep breath. Held it a moment. And roared.

She roared so loud it blew the king's wig off. "I have the soul of a lion!" she cried.

"Again!" the king cried. He flipped the switch himself. Leaned in.

Clara blinked her eyes open.

She hissed. "I am a snake!"

"Madness!" yelled the king. "Again! Again! Again!"

"A hyena! A cougar! A wolf!"

A laugh! A scream! A howl!

"Again!" the king shouted, his voice going hoarse.

It didn't matter. Clara was open now, open to all the souls of the world.

All this time, the beetle patiently worked the tumblers of the heavy lock to the storage tank.

Click click click went the tumblers of the lock. *Click.*

Just one more to go.

Clara was an unstoppable power.

"No!" cried the king.

Click went the final tumbler.

Creak. The door opened and out rushed all the souls of the island.

The king fainted. The guard on duty rushed over—to Clara. He was smiling as he let her go.

15

A FIT OF FIDGETS EVERY SUNDAY

The squirming fidgets started first with Clara Lightbody, but soon spread to the four guests seated around her farmhouse table that Sunday afternoon on the Island of Slippery Souls.

Clara opened her eyes and waited for the others.

"Well," she said, "tell me, tell me."

"A seagull!" sang Ellie.

"A bull," said Ramon.

"A dolphin," smiled Letitia.

"And what about you, Captain Bennick?" asked Ellie.

"Call me Barnacle." The captain bit hard on the stem of his pipe. "Dung beetle. Gonna take some getting used to."

The others laughed.

The captain winked at Ellie. "He's just come from the king."

"And you, Grandma Clara?" asked Ellie.

"Why, I think I have the soul of a tree. Yes, a big shady oak, like the kind that's good for summer picnics."

Clara leaned back in her chair, beaming.

"What?" grinned Ellie.

"Plants, too," said Clara. "It seems the world is full of more souls than we imagined."

She raised her glass of lemonade.

And somewhere out in the sapphire sea, a dolphin with the soul of a hero was swimming, swimming toward a land seen only in the dreams of the people she'd dreamed of, a very strange land where the bodies had never learned to let go of their souls.

Perhaps they could change.

The dolphin chewed her rutabaga and swam on.

320 Sycamore Studios is a scrappy little book company from Seattle.
We make read-aloud stories that are daring, beautiful, and often irreverent.

We publish a new book every three months.

Come join us.

320sycamorestudios.com

ISBN 978-0-9903970-9-0

First Edition

Jeff Williams is a writer who started a little book company in Seattle with some good friends. He carries a pencil and a notebook with him wherever he goes, even when he goes to bed, because you never know when you're going to get an idea for a story. You can reach him at jeff@320sycamorestudios.com.

Katarzyna Surman is an artist and graphic designer who lives in Poland. Her work has appeared in numerous European books and magazines.

Made in the USA
Columbia, SC
16 November 2020

24669094R00049